TOP 10 WOMEN GYMNASTS

Septima Green

SPORTS TOP 10

Enslow Publishers, Inc.
40 Industrial Road   PO Box 38
Box 398   Aldershot
Berkeley Heights, NJ 07922   Hants GU12 6BP
USA   UK
http://www.enslow.com

Copyright © 1999 by Septima Green

All rights reserved.

No part of this book may be reproduced by any means without the written permission of the publisher.

Library of Congress Cataloging-in-Publication Data

Green, Septima.
   Top 10 women gymnasts / Septima Green.
      p. cm. — (Sports top 10)
   Includes bibliographical references (p. 46) and index.
   Summary: Highlights the gymnastic careers of ten of the best women who have competed in the sport: Svetlana Boguinskaia, Vera Caslavska, Nadia Comaneci, Dominique Dawes, Olga Korbut, Larissa Latynina, Shannon Miller, Lilia Podkopayeva, Mary Lou Retton, and Kerri Strug.
     ISBN 0-89490-809-X
   1. Women gymnasts—Biography—Juvenile literature. 2. Women gymnasts—Rating of—Juvenile literature. [1. Gymnasts. 2. Women—Biography.] I. Title. II. Title: Top ten women gymnasts. III. Series.
GV460.G74 1999
796.44'082'0922—dc21
[B]   98-44954
                                                                                                                 CIP
                                                                                                                  AC

Printed in the United States of America

10 9 8 7 6 5 4 3 2 1

To Our Readers:
All Internet addresses in this book were active and appropriate when we went to press. Any comments or suggestions can be sent by e-mail to Comments@enslow.com or to the address on the back cover.

Illustration Credits: Andy Hayt/*Sports Illustrated* © Time, Inc., pp. 38, 41; AP/Wide World Photos, pp. 11, 13, 27, 29, 35, 37; © Cary Garrison, Garrison's Photography, Edmond, Oklahoma, p. 30; Jerry Cooke for *Sports Illustrated* © Time, Inc., p. 23; Nancy Raymond/*International Gymnast*, pp. 9, 19; Neil Leifer for *Sports Illustrated* © Time, Inc., pp. 14, 17; Septima Green, pp. 6, 21, 33, 42, 45; *Sports Illustrated* © Time, Inc., p. 25.

Cover Illustration: © Cary Garrison, Garrison's Photography, Edmond, Oklahoma.

Cover Description: Gold-medal-winning gymnast Shannon Miller.

Interior Design: Richard Stalzer.

CONTENTS

INTRODUCTION	4
SVETLANA BOGUINSKAIA	6
VERA CASLAVSKA	10
NADIA COMANECI	14
DOMINIQUE DAWES	18
OLGA KORBUT	22
LARISSA LATYNINA	26
SHANNON MILLER	30
LILIA PODKOPAYEVA	34
MARY LOU RETTON	38
KERRI STRUG	42
CHAPTER NOTES	46
INDEX	48

Introduction

THE UNITED STATES OLYMPIC COMMITTEE (USOC) received more ticket requests for women's gymnastics than for any other sport of the 1996 Olympic Games. All of the women's gymnastics competitions at the Atlanta Games were performed for standing-room-only crowds. Women's gymnastics received more television coverage than any other sport of the Games. Women's gymnastics is now the most popular Olympic sport.

Gymnastics began over two thousand years ago, and it was one of the sports at the first modern Olympic Games. However, only since the 1952 Games have gymnasts competed for individual as well as team medals.

To compete at an Olympics, the women's gymnastics team must qualify at the World Championships preceding the Games. The top twelve ranking countries then hold trials to select their team members.

Women participate in team, all-around, and individual competition on the vault, uneven bars, balance beam, and floor exercise. Each competitor starts with a 9.4 score from which judges may subtract or add points up to a perfect 10.00.

Most experts and fans agree that Olga Korbut did more than anybody else to popularize gymnastics. She bounced onto the Olympic scene in 1972 and won millions of admirers. Belarus, then part of the Soviet Union, was her home, but people still call her the "mother of American gymnastics." Nadia Comaneci's perfection four years later won still more fans to the sport. And now, because the U.S. "Magnificent Seven" won the team gold medal in Atlanta in 1996, Americans flock to their gymnastics clubs more than ever.

As role models, the athletes in this book encourage young people to try gymnastics. The lessons taught through practicing gymnastics help you feel good about yourself. For participant or fan, gymnastics is a sport to be enjoyed!

Considering the great gymnasts of the past and the many talented ones performing today, selecting the top ten is almost an impossible task. Our choices are partly based on medal count, but also on memorable Olympic performances. Of course, some great athletes had to be left out. Here is *our* list.

OLYMPIC CAREER STATISTICS

Gymnast	Year	Team	All-Around	Vault	Bars	Beam	Floor Exercise	Total
SVETLANA BOGUINSKAIA	1988	Gold	Bronze	Gold			Silver	5
	1992	Gold						
VERA CASLAVSKA	1960	Silver						11
	1964	Silver	Gold	Gold		Gold		
	1968	Silver	Gold	Gold	Gold	Silver	Gold	
NADIA COMANECI	1976	Silver	Gold		Gold	Gold	Bronze	9
	1980	Silver	Bronze			Gold	Gold	
DOMINIQUE DAWES	1992	Bronze						3
	1996	Gold					Bronze	
OLGA KORBUT	1972	Gold			Silver	Gold	Gold	6
	1976	Gold				Silver		
LARISSA LATYNINA	1956	Gold	Gold	Gold	Silver	Bronze	Gold	18
	1960	Gold	Gold	Bronze	Silver	Silver	Gold	
	1964	Gold	Silver	Silver	Bronze	Bronze	Gold	
SHANNON MILLER	1992	Bronze	Silver		Bronze	Silver	Bronze	7
	1996	Gold				Gold		
LILIA PODKOPAYEVA	1996		Gold			Silver	Gold	3
MARY LOU RETTON	1984	Silver	Gold	Silver	Bronze		Bronze	5
KERRI STRUG	1992	Bronze						2
	1996	Gold						

SVETLANA BOGUINSKAIA

In addition to her 5 Olympic medals, Svetlana Boguinskaia has 9 World Championship and 8 European Championship medals.

Svetlana Boguinskaia

A FIFTEEN-YEAR-OLD, hazel-eyed, brunette bowed her head as the Olympic gold medal was placed around her neck. She barely smiled as she acknowledged the crowd's cheers for her perfect vault. The Seoul, South Korea, Olympic spectators saw Svetlana Boguinskaia take the podium four times in the 1988 Games. However, they witnessed little expression or emotion from her or any of her Soviet teammates.

Boguinskaia, who took up gymnastics at age six, was told that this was her job. She should perform well, not only for herself but for her country.

Indeed, her graceful, artistic moves earned much recognition for the former Soviet Union. In 1989, Boguinskaia, known as the Swan, and the Goddess of Gymnastics, won the all-around and floor exercise gold medals at the World Championships. She also won the 1989 and 1990 European titles and became an idol for many young gymnasts.

In 1991, Boguinskaia finished second in the all-around to Kim Zmeskal of the United States at the World Championships. Therefore, prior to the 1992 Olympic Games in Barcelona, Spain, people predicted that the all-around gold would be a close battle between the United States and the Unified Team. The former Soviet Union countries competed in 1992 as the Unified Team. Then, in 1996, they began competing as individual countries.

During the 1992 Olympics, Boguinskaia contributed the most points toward the Unified Team's gold medal. She came close to winning three individual medals as well. She finished fourth in vault and fifth in the all-around and balance beam competitions.

After Barcelona, Boguinskaia retired from competition. She traveled around the world for over a year. In 1994, she arrived in Massachusetts to live with the Freedmans. David Freedman said, "My family fell in love with Svetlana. She even let our twin daughters wear her Olympic medals."[1]

Two and a half years after Boguinskaia declared her retirement, she decided to make a comeback. She asked Bela Karolyi, coach of superstars like Nadia Comaneci, Mary Lou Retton, and Kim Zmeskal, whether he would let her train with him. At first, he resisted. Karolyi thought Boguinskaia was unfriendly—in fact, downright arrogant.[2] The more he got to know her, though, the better he liked her. Finally, he agreed. Boguinskaia moved to Houston and began the most successful comeback of any gymnast who had been away from competition for such a long time.

Boguinskaia won second place, behind Kerri Strug, in the 1996 American Cup. She went on to Birmingham, England for the European Championships. She almost pulled off an upset, but she settled for the silver all-around medal. She claimed a spot for her third Olympic Games in Atlanta and helped her native Belarus place sixth in the team competition. She also qualified for the vault finals and came in fifth.

International Gymnast magazine said, "With so many athletes proclaiming their comebacks, it's nice to see that Svetlana is really doing it and with incredible style."[3]

Svetlana Boguinskaia claims that gymnastics will always have a place in her life and that she enjoys it more than ever now that she is doing it for fun. She certainly has come a long way from being the serious girl on the podium!

SVETLANA BOGUINSKAIA

BORN: February 9, 1973, Minsk, Belarus.

GYMNASTICS CLUBS: Soviet Training Center near Moscow; Karolyi's and Brown's in Houston, Texas.

COACHES: Lyubov Miromanova, Bela Karolyi, and Alexander Alexandrov.

FAVORITE APPARATUS: Balance beam.

HONORS/AWARDS: All-around World Champion, 1989; floor exercise World Champion, 1989 (tie); balance beam World Champion, 1991.

Although the balance beam was her favorite event, Boguinskaia won gold medals on all four apparatuses.

Internet Address
http://www.usa-gymnastics.org/athletes/intlbios/b/sboguinskaia.html

Vera Caslavska

VERA CASLAVSKA OF CZECHOSLOVAKIA and Larissa Petrick of the Soviet Union stood side by side in the center atop the white Olympic podium in 1968. The women waved to the cheering crowd that filled the Mexico City National Auditorium. Caslavska smiled while the Czech national anthem played, but her smile faded, and she looked down as the Soviet national anthem played.

Two months before, the Soviet Union had invaded her homeland. She believed politics affected the way judges were scoring some Olympic events. Already a controversy had taken place regarding her silver medal on the balance beam. Now, in the final event, Caslavska engaged the audience throughout her flawless floor exercise, earning a 9.9. She had expected the gold medal to be hers alone; yet, prior to the victory ceremony, officials revised Larissa Petrick's score to match Caslavska's.

Caslavska overcame these problems and was hailed as Queen of the Games in Mexico City.[1] For the third consecutive Olympics, she led Czechoslovakia's women's gymnastics team to the silver medal—trailing the Soviet Union by only 0.65 of a point.

She also became the second of only two female gymnasts to win two Olympic all-around titles. She was the first woman in any sport to take four individual gold medals in a single Olympics. Caslavska became the only female athlete in any sport who has seven individual Olympic gold medals.

To win the all-around title, Caslavska executed exciting moves on the uneven bars, a standing split known as the

In a ten-year span, Vera Caslavska won 22 gold medals in major gymnastics competitions. She was the first gymnast to sweep two European championships.

VERA CASLAVSKA

needle scale on the balance beam, a "Yamashita" vault, and a thrilling floor routine to the music of the "Mexican Hat Dance." The people of Mexico adored her, and fellow gymnasts did as well. Her teammates and opponents crowded around the two-time champion, lifted her high into the air, and cheered.

The day after the gymnastics competition ended, Caslavska added further excitement to the 1968 Games by getting married. More than ten thousand fans surrounded the church where Caslavska and Czechoslovakian track medalist Josef Odlozil exchanged vows.

In 1968, the Soviet Union had sent troops into Czechoslovakia. Caslavska had resisted Soviet control of her country, and because of this she could not train in a proper facility. She had to practice her floor exercise in a meadow, and use tree limbs as bars. This is why her performance is considered to be so incredible.

By special invitation, Caslavska spent two years coaching the Mexican national gymnastics team. Caslavska had won her first Olympic title in Tokyo, Japan. Through the years, the Japanese government also has continued to seek her advice and used her as a role model.

In 1992, she became president of the Czech National Olympic Committee. An interviewer asked her if she loved her sport as much as ever. She replied, "It will be with me all my life."[2]

Vera Caslavska showed bravery both in her work on gym apparatuses and in her political decisions. It is no wonder that people around the world respect and admire her as both an athlete and a person.

VERA CASLAVSKA

BORN: May 3, 1942, Prague, Czechoslovakia.
GYMNASTICS CLUBS: Slovan Prague; Red Star.
COACHES: Vladimir Prorok and Eva Bosakova.
FAVORITE APPARATUS: Vault.
HONORS/AWARDS: All-around World Champion, 1966; vault World Champion, 1962, 1966; inducted into International Gymnastics Hall of Fame, 1998; president of Czech National Olympic Committee; received offers to be Ambassador of Sport from both Japan and Mexico.

Besides excelling at gymnastics, Caslavska was a former figure skater, held jobs in government and in the Olympic administration, and was an accomplished oil painter.

NADIA COMANECI

In 1975, at age thirteen, Nadia Comaneci surprised everyone at the European Championships. At that competition she beat reigning World and Olympic champion Ludmilla Touricheva.

Nadia Comaneci

"**Now Entering The Arena** for the 1976 Olympic Games—the Romanian team!" resounded the speaker for the second time.

"Sir," fourteen-year-old Nadia Comaneci whispered to her coach, "they're calling us. Shouldn't we go in?"[1]

Bela Karolyi, wanting to get the audience's attention, held his team back for a few more moments. He knew there was a direct relationship between audience support and high scores. Then he gave his team the go-ahead.

Looking like tiny dolls, they marched into the Montreal Forum, wearing white leotards with red piping down the sides and matching bows in their hair. Indeed, the spectators and the media noticed the Romanians. The gymnasts' polished routines kept everyone's attention.

In her compulsory bar routine, Comaneci flew like a bird through the air with style and extensions no one had seen before. As she stuck her dismount, the crowd broke into wild cheering and clapping. They grew silent, though, when they saw the scoreboard display a 1.00.

"What kind of a score is that?" people wondered. Good scores ranged upward from 9.70.

An announcement from the speaker erased the confusion. "Ladies and gentlemen, for the first time in Olympic history, Nadia Comaneci has received the score of a perfect ten." The scoreboard did not have room to accommodate a two-digit number before the decimal.

Comaneci dazzled the audience with perfection six more times in the 1976 Games and is the only Romanian ever to win the all-around title. She replaced Olga Korbut as the new darling of women's gymnastics.

It all began in Onesti, Romania, at an elementary school, when Comaneci was six years old. Bela Karolyi was recruiting gymnasts for his school when he saw two little blond-haired girls doing cartwheels in the corner of a playground. The bell rang, and all the children dashed inside so fast, Karolyi lost track of the girls. He looked in every classroom and was almost ready to give up when he saw them again.[2]

Comaneci and her friend joined Karolyi's gymnastics program. Karolyi said Comaneci was quiet and didn't stand out in the beginning. The trait that did impress Karolyi was the fact that she never said "No" or "I can't do that." This quality enabled her to progress rapidly.[3]

Although gymnastics occupied most of her time as a child, Comaneci loved to go fishing with her brother or go to their grandmother's house. There, they climbed cherry trees and picked cherries.[4]

Her life has not always been perfect, though. In 1978, she experienced burnout and gained forty pounds. With Comaneci's determination and Karolyi's rugged training, she came back to provide the world with two more years of inspiring performances.

A scary time for Comaneci was when she escaped from her Communist-controlled country in 1989. Comaneci settled in Oklahoma, where she became acquainted with Bart Conner. Conner was also an Olympic gold medal winner, and he and Comaneci had a lot in common. On April 27, 1996, Comaneci and Conner were married in Bucharest, Romania.

Today at their Norman, Oklahoma home they operate a gymnastics academy, produce and perform in gymnastics exhibitions around the world, and donate much time and money to charities.

NADIA COMANECI

BORN: November 12, 1961, Onesti, Romania.

EDUCATION: Physical Education and Sport Institute in Bucharest, Romania.

GYMNASTICS CLUB: Romanian Gymnastics Federation.

COACHES: Bela and Marta Karolyi.

FAVORITE APPARATUS: Uneven bars and balance beam.

HONORS: Balance beam World Champion, 1978; Associated Press Female Athlete of the Year, 1976; IOC Olympic Order Award, 1984; Sudafed International Women's Sports Hall of Fame, 1991; inducted into International Gymnastics Hall of Fame, 1993; named honorary president of Romanian Gymnastics Federation, 1996; honored in Atlanta's Opening Ceremonies as an unforgettable Olympian, 1996.

The youngest all-around champion in Olympic history, Comaneci's beautiful and flawless gymnastics at the 1976 Montreal Games may never be duplicated or surpassed.

Internet Address
http://www.netsrq.com/~dbois/comaneci.htm

Dominique Dawes

DOMINIQUE DAWES WANTED an individual Olympic medal. Her chances looked good. She was the only American gymnast with four chances for an individual medal in the 1996 Olympic Games. At the 1992 Games, she had helped her team win the bronze medal but failed to qualify for any individual finals.

In Atlanta, things already were going well. On July 23, 1996, Dawes helped her team take the gold medal. The women's team celebrated at Planet Hollywood as the guests of actors Bruce Willis and Demi Moore.

Two days later, still high from their victory, Dawes, Shannon Miller, and Dominique Moceanu prepared to compete in the all-around finals. (Moceanu had replaced the injured Kerri Strug.) By the third rotation, Dawes was in first place and Miller was second out of thirty-six finalists. The crowd grew wildly excited, but soon their hopes crumbled when Miller stepped out of bounds during her floor exercise. Then Dawes fell out of bounds on the same event. Their hopes for a medal slipped away. Miller placed eighth, Moceanu placed ninth, and Dawes finished in a tie for seventeenth.

Now Dawes would have to overcome that disappointing performance, because she still had three individual apparatus finals to go. On Sunday night, she came in sixth in the vault competition and fourth on the uneven bars.

Monday, the final night of gymnastics competition, Dawes replaced Kerri Strug in the floor exercise. Kelli Hill, Dawes's lifetime coach, encouraged her to forget the all-around competition and to focus on this one last

DOMINIQUE DAWES

Dominique Dawes swept the 1994 USA Nationals, becoming the first person in twenty-five years to collect all five of the gold medals.

opportunity to get her medal. A confident Dawes tumbled her way into the hearts of the audience and the judges, earning a 9.825 and the bronze medal.

Hill said, "Dominique acquired the nickname of 'Awesome Dawesome' because her gymnastics were indeed awesome."[1]

Her reputation for fantastic floor exercises began in 1992 when she scored a perfect 10.00 at the dual competition between the United States and Japan. She went on to become only the second African-American gymnast to earn a spot on the United States women's Olympic team. She became the first African American to win individual World Championship medals in gymnastics, winning two silvers and placing fourth all-around at the 1993 Worlds in Birmingham, England. The next year, in Brisbane, Australia, she placed fifth in the all-around and qualified for three event finals. Although she made the 1995 world team, injuries kept her from going to Sabae, Japan. Then she brought home an individual bronze medal from the 1996 World Championships in Puerto Rico.

Perhaps most impressive is the fact that she has fifteen gold national championship medals—more than any other United States gymnast, male or female.

Dominique Dawes has made gymnastics history and continues to touch the lives of young people. Hill said, "She cheers on other little girls in the gym. It doesn't matter what level or age they are."[2] In her Washington, D.C., area, Dawes visits schools, warning children about the dangers of drugs.

When United States Gymnastics public relations director Luan Peszek asked the Magnificent Seven, "Who is the most exciting person you've met since the '96 Games?" other team members cited various celebrities. But Dawes replied, "The most exciting people definitely are the young fans."[3]

Dominique Dawes

BORN: November 20, 1976, Silver Spring, Maryland.

EDUCATION: Gaithersburg High School, Gaithersburg, Maryland; University of Maryland.

GYMNASTICS CLUB: Hill's Gymnastics, Gaithersburg, Maryland.

COACH: Kelli Hill.

FAVORITE APPARATUS: All.

HONORS/AWARDS: USA Gymnastics Athlete of the Year, 1993; top ten finalist for James E. Sullivan Award, 1994; USA Gymnastics Sportsperson of the Year, 1994; *Sports Illustrated for Kids* Good Sport Award, 1995; Arch McDonald Award, 1995; Henry P. Iba Citizen Award, 1995.

In middle school, Dawes developed her 3-D philosophy for success. The 3-D's: Determination, Dedication, and Dynamics continue to inspire her to do her best.

Internet Address
http://www.usa-gymnastics.org/athletes/bios/d/ddawes.html

Olga Korbut

NOTHING COULD PREPARE the spectators in the Sporthalle in Munich, Germany, or the television viewers around the world for what they were about to witness. It was August 28, the second day of the women's gymnastics team competition during the 1972 Olympic Games. The previous day, teams from the nineteen participating countries had performed compulsory routines—routines required by the judges—but today the women had a chance to demonstrate their individual creativity and special talents.

The Soviet Union's team began competing in the floor exercise. The audience noticed one pixie of a girl, Olga Korbut, who smiled as she skipped like a sparrow through her routine. On the second rotation, they liked Korbut's high Yamashita vault.

Next, the Soviets went to the uneven bars. Korbut took her turn and performed a trick no one had ever seen in competitive gymnastics. Standing on the high bar, she did a back flip, then regrasped the bar! The stunned audience couldn't believe their eyes, and continued to applaud after Korbut sat down with her coaches and teammates. She stood up again and waved her hands high in the air to the people on both sides of the Sporthalle.

On the balance beam in the final rotation, Korbut continued to excite her audience. She whirled backwards into the air, yet landed gracefully on the apparatus.

The day ended with the Soviets winning the team gold medal and Korbut placing third among all the women gymnasts in the world.

Newspapers around the world wrote about the petite,

OLGA KORBUT

When Olga Korbut was fourteen and the age requirement sixteen, Korbut became the youngest person to ever make the USSR's national team.

seventeen-year-old pigtailed girl who was revolutionizing gymnastics.

Two days later, fans eagerly awaited Korbut's all-around performances. The audience adored her playful, yet polished, floor routine. They gave her thunderous applause, and the judges gave her the highest score of the first round—a 9.8. After the second rotation, Korbut held on to first place.

She was having the time of her life. Smiling, she approached the bars. But as she jumped forward to begin her kip, disaster struck. The kip is a move in which the gymnast flips from a hanging position to a position above the bar. As she swung, the soles of her feet rubbed against the floor, almost stopping her forward motion.[1] She started again, but she had lost her focus, and she made two other mistakes. Bewilderment replaced her normally bubbly attitude. She held back her tears long enough to acknowledge the judges, but returned to her coach shaking with sobs. The judges gave her a 7.5, ending her chances of an all-around medal.

Later that night, Korbut told television reporters, "I won't make any more blunders. I simply won't."[2] The next day she proved that she could bounce back. In the apparatus finals, she took gold medals on the beam and floor exercise, as well as a silver on the uneven bars. Few athletes in any sport have captured the world's heart the way Korbut did in Munich.

Olga Korbut officially retired in 1977, married folksinger Leonid Bortkevich in 1978, and gave birth to their son, Richard, in 1979. Today they live in Georgia, in the United States, where Korbut coaches gymnastics and works to help victims of the Chernobyl nuclear disaster.

Olga Korbut

BORN: May 16, 1955, Grodno, Belarus.

EDUCATION: Institute of Pedagogics in Grodno, Belarus.

GYMNASTICS CLUB: Soviet Training Center.

COACH: Renald Knysh.

FAVORITE APPARATUS: All.

HONORS/AWARDS: Soviet Gymnastics Federation Master of Sport award, 1972; guest of President Nixon at the White House, 1973; Associated Press Female Athlete of the Year, 1973; vault World Champion, 1974; honored with Moscow Tribute to Olga, 1978; first person inducted into the International Gymnastics Hall of Fame, 1988; selected by *Sports Illustrated* as the gymnast who has made the all-time greatest impact on the sport, 1994.

In between the Olympic years of 1972 and 1976, Korbut continued to win gold medals. She won 5 medals at the 1974 World Championships.

Internet Address
http://www.netsrq.com/~dbois/korbut.html

Larissa Latynina

LARISSA LATYNINA OF THE FORMER Soviet Union has more Olympic medals than any other athlete in any sport. She also has set more Olympic records than anyone else.

Latynina, a solid competitor in three consecutive Olympics, won a total of 18 medals. Her 9 gold medals are the most won by a woman, and only three men in history have that many. Only one other woman gymnast has won back-to-back all-around Olympic gold medals, and no other female gymnast has won three all-around medals. Also, no other female has won three Olympic gold medals for the same individual apparatus final.

In the 1950s and 1960s, World Championships were held every four years. Latynina dominated gymnastics titles by winning the 1956 Olympics, 1958 Worlds, 1960 Olympics, and 1962 Worlds. In the 1964 Olympics, she slipped into second place when Vera Caslavska won.

Latynina was born in the Ukraine. She became a member of the Soviet national team at nineteen. The Soviet system of training gymnasts was superior to that of any other country in Europe or the rest of the world. Latynina's training under Coach Alexander Mishakov gave her an edge over foreign competitors.

The level of difficulty of gymnastics at that time caused less physical stress, and there was less chance of injury than there is today. This allowed women to compete longer. Execution of gymnastics skills, however, certainly did require intensive training, discipline, and effort. Latynina, orphaned and poor as a child, knew how to make sacrifices and dedicate herself to the sport.

Larissa Latynina was known for her fabulous floor exercises. She won 3 individual Olympic gold medals in that event.

LARISSA LATYNINA

Throughout her life, she has striven for excellence. Beyond her own gymnastics accomplishments, she served for ten years as senior coach of the USSR (Union of Soviet Socialist Republics) national women's team. She nurtured and guided the team through three Olympic championships. She is especially remembered for the 1972 team she created, which included greats such as Olga Korbut and Ludmilla Touricheva.

In 1976, Latynina's team won the gold, but a young Romanian woman by the name of Nadia Comaneci won the all-around title. The Soviet leaders, used to winning everything, thought Latynina was not doing her job as well as she should. They wanted to see gymnastics supertricks, as opposed to the elegant artistry Latynina taught. She resigned from the national post and later took a job heading the Moscow women's team.[1]

In 1989, the International Olympic Committee presented Latynina the Olympic Order award for her service and dedication to her sport. As a participant and coach for thirty-six years of her life, she certainly deserved the honor.

Today Latynina and her husband live in a small Moscow apartment. They enjoy playing tennis on their own court or spending time with their children and grandchildren.[2]

Larissa Latynina's legacy to gymnastics will never be surpassed.

LARISSA LATYNINA

BORN: December 27, 1934, Kherson, Ukraine.
EDUCATION: Kiev State Institute of Physical Culture.
GYMNASTICS CLUB: Soviet National Training Center.
COACH: Alexander Mishakov.
FAVORITE APPARATUS: Floor exercise.
HONORS/AWARDS: All-around World Champion, 1958, 1962; floor exercise World Champion, 1962; uneven bars World Champion, 1958; balance beam World Champion, 1958; vault World Champion, 1958; named overall director of gymnastics competitions for 1980 Olympic Games; Olympic Order Award by International Olympic Committee, 1989; inducted into the International Gymnastics Hall of Fame, 1998.

Through the 1998 Games, Latynina's 18 Olympic medals have not been matched by any other athlete, man or woman.

Shannon Miller's five medals at the 1992 Games were more than any other American athlete competing in the Olympics that year.

Shannon Miller

LATE MONDAY EVENING, July 29, 1996, a hushed, sold-out crowd of thirty-two thousand people watched Shannon Miller's pressed handstand as she mounted the balance beam. She took control of the four-inch-wide apparatus, pirouetting, leaping, and flipping her way through a practically flawless routine. When she stuck her spectacular dismount, the audience (mainly Americans) burst into thunderous applause.

Tension mounted in the Georgia Dome. Romanian Alexandra Marinescu had fallen twice during that event. Dominique Moceanu, Miller's teammate, also fell. Russian Dina Kochetkova, the 1995 world beam champion, made a slight error. The judges had awarded Miller a 9.862, which would be hard to beat. But this was the Olympics, and anything could happen.

Next up, the all-around World and Olympic champion, Ukrainian Lilia Podkopayeva, gave an impressive routine. The audience held its breath. Then the results flashed on the scoreboard. Podkopayeva had received a 9.825. Miller still led the competition!

Three others tried to crack Miller's score. Last up, European beam champion Rozalia Galiyeva of Russia fell, bringing the audience to its feet. Now they knew for sure the gold belonged to Miller and to the United States!

That night in Atlanta, Miller told reporters, "I was pleased I hit my routine and did a good job. I knew it was a good note to end on no matter what color the medal was."[1]

By "a good note to end on," Miller meant that this balance

beam routine was probably her last Olympic performance. It was the thirtieth performance of her Olympic career.

Six days before winning her individual gold, Miller led the U.S. women's team to its first gold medal in Olympic history. Helping the team win this medal had been a long-time goal. Before the Olympics, she said, "The all-around or an individual medal in Atlanta would be really exciting, but I want the team gold even more."[2]

Each time Miller has participated in an Olympic or World team competition, she has contributed the most points for the United States. Many people are unaware of the sacrifice she made for the team at the 1995 World Championships in Sabae, Japan. After compulsories, she was in third place. Unfortunately, she injured her right ankle during a beam dismount, but she kept competing through the later rounds. If she had not continued in the optional competition, the United States definitely would have lost the bronze medal to Russia.

"She's a fighter!" claimed Steve Nunno, Miller's coach. In 1986, Nunno happened to attend a Moscow seminar while the members of Miller's recreational gym observed Russian gymnasts. He said he admired her determination to attempt "hard skills the Russian coaches were literally throwing her through."[3]

In spite of injuries and upsets, no American gymnast has a record even close to Miller's. She holds 2 United States National Championship titles, 2 back-to-back World Championship titles, and many others. She has a total of 16 World Championship and Olympic medals.

Now Miller's thousands of fans can still see her on the annual Tour of World Gymnastics Champions and in competitions like the World Professional Championships or the Reese's Gymnastics Cup. Miller will stay involved in the sport she loves so much.

Shannon Miller

BORN: March 10, 1977, Rolla, Missouri.

EDUCATION: Edmond North High School, Edmond, Oklahoma; University of Oklahoma.

GYMNASTICS CLUB: Dynamo Gymnastics, Oklahoma City, Oklahoma.

COACHES: Steve Nunno and Peggy Liddick.

FAVORITE APPARATUS: Balance beam and uneven bars.

HONORS/AWARDS: All-around World Champion, 1993–94; floor exercise World Champion, 1993; uneven bars World Champion, 1993; balance beam World Champion, 1994; Master of Sport Award by USA Gymnastics, 1993; Athlete of the Year for Women's Artistic Gymnastics by United States Olympic Committee, 1993–94; Henry P. Iba Citizen Athlete Award, 1994; Dial Award for Most Outstanding Female Athlete/Scholar, 1994; top ten finalist for James E. Sullivan Award, 1993–95; portion of Interstate 35 in Oklahoma renamed Shannon Miller Parkway, 1998.

Miller placed priority on her education throughout her gymnastics career. Despite her hectic schedule, she was able to attend public schools and graduate high school on time with her class.

Internet Address

http://www.usa-gymnastics.org/athletes/bios/m/smiller.html

Lilia Podkopayeva

ON THE AFTERNOON OF July 25, 1996, a rowdy Georgia Dome crowd seemed even more spirited than they had been during the team competition. The all-around women's gymnastics championship was at stake, and this audience expected one of the three Americans to win.

Gymnasts, as part of their training, learn to tune out distractions. But the noise and confusion bothered many of the thirty-six finalists. Lilia Podkopayeva of the Ukraine previously had performed for calm European and Asian audiences. "I told myself not to pay attention," she said. "At the beginning, I wasn't used to it, but I learned to adapt by concentrating."[1]

Podkopayeva, who posted the highest individual score in team competition over ninety-five other women gymnasts, got off to a slower start in the all-around. Her vault earned a respectable 9.781, but Russia's Rozalia Galiyeva led the first round. Dominique Dawes of the United States pressed ahead of everyone by the end of round two. The third rotation produced yet another pair of leaders—Russia's Dina Kochetkova and China's Mo Huilan. Podkopayeva, however, had inched into third place.

Luckily for Podkopayeva, she drew for last her favorite and best event—the floor exercise. The American audiences ended up loving Podkopayeva! They clapped to her music and even approved of her 9.887 score. Podkopayeva finally led the all-around competition. Huilan still had her floor exercise to go. When it was Huilan's turn, she stepped out of bounds, leaving the gold for Podkopayeva.

On the podium, Podkopayeva experienced mixed

LILIA PODKOPAYEVA

Lilia Podkopayeva proved her superiority in the gymnastics world by being World, European, and Olympic champion all at once. She was the first person to do that since 1972.

emotions. She cried when the medal was placed around her neck. Only four weeks before, the grandmother who introduced her to gymnastics had died. She kissed the medal and dedicated it to her beloved grandmother. As the Ukrainian national anthem played, she bravely stood and waved her bouquet of flowers to the crowd.

Podkopayeva also qualified for three individual apparatus finals. Her uneven bars routine contained difficult skills and was beautifully executed, but she failed to stick her dismount, giving her a tie for fifth place. She won the silver medal for her beam performance. Four floor exercise finalists had scored a 9.8 or better. This meant if Podkopayeva wanted the gold, she'd have to be practically perfect. She was! Podkopayeva scored a 9.887.

The three Olympic medals Podkopayeva won in Atlanta fulfilled a longtime ambition for her. Although she was five years old when her grandmother first took her to a gym, she was fourteen before she entered major competitions. She entered her first World Competition in 1993 in Birmingham, England, and qualified for the vault finals. In the 1994 Worlds, she qualified for three apparatus finals and won the silver medal for her balance beam performance. In 1995, she became World Champion in Sabae, Japan.

After the Olympics she said, "Winning in Sabae was a big surprise and a shock. But the major dream of my life was to win the Olympic Games."[2]

Podkopayeva is happy with the recognition her country has given her since the Olympics, but she has concerns about continuing in competitive gymnastics. She wants to be remembered at her best, not like those who stay beyond their prime. She should not worry about anyone thinking of Lilia Podkopayeva as anything other than a champion gymnast.

LILIA PODKOPAYEVA

BORN: August 15, 1978, Donetsk, Ukraine.
GYMNASTICS CLUB: Ukrainian School of Gymnastics.
COACH: Galina Losinskaya.
FAVORITE APPARATUS: Floor exercise.
HONORS/AWARDS: All-around World Champion, 1995; vault World Champion (tie), 1995; finalist for Women's Sports Foundation Sportswoman of the Year, 1996; Selected for Tour of World Gymnastics Champions, 1996–97.

Podkopayeva's two 9.887 marks in the floor exercise were the highest recorded marks of the women's gymnastics competitions at the 1996 Summer Olympics.

Internet Address
http://www.usa-gymnastics.org/athletes/intlbios/p/
lpodkopayeva.html

MARY LOU RETTON

In March 1985, Mary Lou Retton became the first woman to win three consecutive McDonald's American Cup championships.

Mary Lou Retton

Nine Thousand People in the Los Angeles Pauley Pavilion held still. They realized that Olympic history could be in the making at the 1984 Summer Games.

Reigning World Champion Ecaterina Szabo of Romania led the women's all-around competition. She had a 0.05 edge over Mary Lou Retton of the United States as they entered the final event. Ecaterina performed her uneven bars routine beautifully except for taking a big step on her dismount. She scored a 9.90. Now came the time for Retton's vault. Bela Karolyi, her coach, hollered, "Here's the vault of your life! It's now or never! Stick it!" He knew only a perfect ten would allow Retton to win.

Millions of television viewers around the world watched the sixteen-year-old girl jog in place as she waited for the green light. At the signal, she sprinted down the runway and bounced off the springboard with a force that literally sent her sailing upside down, vertically, into the air. All the while, her legs were perfectly together, and she landed solidly.

No one waited to see the score. Retton, Karolyi, and the spectators all knew it had to be a 10.00. Retton's arms went up as if she were a referee signaling a touchdown. Karolyi shouted, "Olympic champion!" and the crowd gave Retton a standing ovation.

No American woman had ever won an individual Olympic medal in gymnastics and certainly not the best prize of all, the all-around gold. "This is the moment I worked nine years for," Retton told herself.[1]

Some people do not realize what Retton had to go

through to be able to compete at the 1984 games. Retton had knee surgery only six weeks before the Olympics. Her strong determination to build endurance and get back into condition allowed her to go to the Games.

Once she was there, Retton's charisma captured the audience as much as her upbeat, yet powerful, gymnastics. The only gymnast in Los Angeles who qualified for every event final, she won a silver and two bronze medals to add to her team silver and all-around gold.

The pint-sized dynamo from Fairmont, West Virginia, was the baby of her family. At seven, she and her sister began taking gymnastics lessons for fun. But at eight, as she sat on her living room floor watching Nadia Comaneci at the 1976 Olympics, she said, "Mom, I want to be just like Nadia, and I want to be in the Olympics."

"Sure, honey, sure," her mom replied.[2]

Retton held on to that dream. She made the junior national team when she was thirteen and won her first international competition in Canada. She moved to Houston on New Year's Day 1983 to train with Bela Karolyi, the man who had coached Nadia Comaneci to her Olympic glory.

At first Karolyi worried about Retton's easygoing personality, but her disposition proved to be an asset. Of all the world-class gymnasts he had coached, Karolyi claimed, "Mary Lou was the sunshine of Marta's and my career."[3]

She still shines today—over a decade since her championship days. She continues to get endorsement contracts and give motivational speeches.

Although her husband, Shannon Kelley, and their daughters, Shayla Rae and McKenna Lane, are Retton's priorities today, she'll always be an ambassador for her sport.

Mary Lou Retton

BORN: January 24, 1968, Fairmont, West Virginia.

EDUCATION: Correspondence courses and private school; attended the University of Texas.

GYMNASTICS CLUB: Karolyi's, Houston, Texas.

COACHES: Gary Rafaloski; Bela and Marta Karolyi.

FAVORITE APPARATUS: Floor exercise, vault.

HONORS/AWARDS: Associated Press and *Sports Illustrated* Sportswoman of the Year, 1984; USA Gymnastics Federation Hall of Fame, 1985; Sudafed International Women's Sports Hall of Fame, 1993; national chairperson for Children's Miracle Network; Flo Hyman Award, 1995; USOC established the annual Mary Lou Retton Award for athletic achievement, 1995; inducted into International Gymnastics Hall of Fame, 1997.

Sports Illustrated declared this "The Vault without Fault!" after Retton's perfect score. Her success at the 1984 Olympics made her so famous that General Mills cereal company chose her as the first woman athlete to appear on the Wheaties box.

Internet Address
http://www.olympic-usa.org/games/ga_2_5_71.html

KERRI STRUG

Kerri Strug had to withdraw from the all-around and individual event competitions due to the injury she sustained during her vault. However, her vault was a moment that truly captured the Olympic spirit.

Kerri Strug

ONLY THE VAULT REMAINED. For the first time in Olympic or World Championship history, the United States women's gymnastics team led the team competition against every other country in the world. Kerri Strug and her six teammates approached the fourth and final rotation of the 1996 Olympic Games. The United States' lead was less than one full-point over second-place Russia and ranked slightly over a point ahead of third-place Romania.

In the 1996 Olympic team competition, six of the seven United States team members competed in each event with only the five highest scores counting. Jaycie Phelps, Amy Chow, Shannon Miller, and Dominique Dawes performed acceptable vaults. Fifth up, Dominique Moceanu landed on her backside on both of her vaults.

The cries of, "USA! USA!" hushed. People began to worry. The Russians, still participating in the floor exercise, had saved one of their best, Rozalia Galiyeva, for last. Surely the final U.S. vaulter, Kerri Strug, would make things all right.

Strug felt extreme pressure as she ran toward the horse. Unfortunately, she also fell. Was the gold medal going to slip away in the last few moments of a two-day competition?

What onlookers didn't know was that Strug had heard a *pop* in her left ankle. When she stood, a fiery pain shot up her leg. She knew she was hurt but thought the gold medal depended on her second vault. She heard her coach, Bela Karolyi, yell to her, "You can do it!"[1]

In spite of the pain, the adrenaline began to race in her blood as she agreed with Karolyi, "I can do this. I've done it a million times." She said a prayer: "Please, God, help me out here."[2]

Incredibly, Strug performed her Yurchenko vault with one and a half twists, and she stuck her landing on both feet. As she saluted the judges, her left leg lifted in throbbing pain. Then she crumpled to the mat.

Mixed emotions ran rampant in the dome—concern for Strug's injury and elation over the United States team victory. Medics prepared to take Strug to the hospital. When she begged to stay for the medal presentation, Karolyi lifted her off the stretcher and carried her to the podium. "The Star Spangled Banner" played, and the United States flag was raised as Strug stood on one leg alongside her teammates. Tears sprang into her eyes as she received her precious gold medal.

The Russian's final scores had not been posted at the time of Strug's second vault. Therefore, few realized the United States already had enough points to win the gold medal. Still, Strug's courage will always be an unforgettable moment in Olympic history.

It took every girl's effort to win the team medal, but the media made Strug a heroine overnight. Although she'd been giving solid gymnastics performances for years, Strug had never been in the spotlight.

Strug has always believed in herself and her teammates. Nine months before the Olympics, when others were predicting that the women's team would win bronze or silver at best, she said, "We can win the team gold in Atlanta. We have our work cut out for us, but if we have our top people healthy, we can win."[3]

Kerri Strug

BORN: November 19, 1977, Tucson, Arizona.

EDUCATION: Northland Christian School, Houston, Texas; Green Fields Country Day High School in Tucson, Arizona; University of California at Los Angeles.

GYMNASTICS CLUBS: Karolyi's, Houston, Texas; Dynamo, Oklahoma City, Oklahoma; Colorado Aerials, Colorado Springs, Colorado.

COACHES: Bela and Marta Karolyi.

FAVORITE APPARATUS: Floor exercise.

HONORS: Guest at President Bill Clinton's fiftieth birthday party; tossed the coin at the beginning of the Dallas Cowboys vs. the Philadelphia Eagles football game.

Strug was the 1996 American Cup champion, and winner of two apparatus finals. Strug gave up seven thousand dollars worth of prize money so that she could compete in the Summer Olympics.

Internet Address

http://www.usa-gymnastics.org/athletes/bios/s/kstrug.html

Chapter Notes

Svetlana Boguinskaia
1. Septima Green, phone interview with David Freedman, Needham, Mass., June 1996.
2. Mark McDonald, "Boguinskaia's Routine Regains Lost Balance," *The Dallas Morning News*, March 3, 1996, sec. B, p. 26.
3. Paul Ziert, "Keeping Pace with Olympic Race," *International Gymnast*, vol. 38, no. 4, April 1996, p. 6.

Vera Caslavska
1. Bud Greenspan, *100 Greatest Moments in Olympic History* (Santa Monica, Calif.: General Publishing Group, Inc., 1995), p. 51.
2. Minot Simons, II, *Women's Gymnastics: A History*, vol. 1 (Carmel, Calif.: Welwyn Publishing Company, 1995), p. 117.

Nadia Comaneci
1. Bela Karolyi with Nancy Ann Richardson, *Feel No Fear* (New York: Hyperion, 1994), p. 59.
2. Ibid., p. 43.
3. Ibid., p. 44.
4. Nadia Comaneci, "Ask Bart and Nadia," *International Gymnast*, vol. 39, no. 5, May 1997, p. 43.

Dominique Dawes
1. Septima Green, phone interview with Kelli Hill, Gaithersburg, Md., March 22, 1996.
2. Ibid.
3. Luan Peszek, "What's Happening with the Mag 7!," *USA Gymnastics*, vol. 25, no. 6, November/December 1996, p. 29.

Olga Korbut
1. Minot Simons, II, *Women's Gymnastics: A History*, vol. 1 (Carmel, Calif.: Welwyn Publishing Company, 1995), pp. 230–231.
2. Justin Beecham, *Olga: Her Life and Her Gymnastics* (New York: Paddington Press Ltd, 1974), p. 102.

Larissa Latynina
1. Minot Simons, II, *Women's Gymnastics: A History*, vol. 1 (Carmel, Calif.: Welwyn Publishing Company, 1995), p. 106.
2. Larissa Latynina's acceptance speech, Second Annual International Gymnastics Hall of Fame induction ceremony, Oklahoma City, June 26, 1998.

Shannon Miller
1. Terry Tush, "Striking Gold Again," *Edmond Evening Sun*, vol. 107, no. 150, July 30, 1996, sec. A, p. 1.
2. Septima Green, personal interview with Shannon Miller, Edmond, Okla., September 1, 1995.
3. Septima Green, *Going for the Gold: Shannon Miller* (New York: Avon Books, 1996), p. 22.

Lilia Podkopayeva
1. John Crumlish, "For the Love of Lilia," *International Gymnast*, vol. 38, no. 12, December 1996, p. 10.
2. Ibid.

Mary Lou Retton
1. Mary Lou Retton and Bela Karolyi with John Powers, *Mary Lou: Creating an Olympic Champion* (New York: McGraw-Hill Book Company, 1986), p. 160.
2. Mary Lou Retton's acceptance speech, International Gymnastics Hall of Fame induction ceremony, Oklahoma City, June 27, 1997.
3. Bela Karolyi with Nancy Ann Richardson, *Feel No Fear* (New York: Hyperion, 1994), p. 140.

Kerri Strug
1. Kerri Strug with Greg Brown, *Heart of Gold* (Dallas: Taylor Publishing, 1996), p. 40.
2. Ibid.
3. Septima Green, phone interview with Kerri Strug, Colorado Springs, Col., October 24, 1995.

INDEX

A
American Cup, 8

B
Boguinskaia, Svetlana, 6–9

C
Caslavska, Vera, 10–13
Chow, Amy, 43
Comaneci, Nadia, 4, 14–17, 28, 40
Conner, Bart, 16
Czech National Olympic Committee, 12

D
Dawes, Dominique, 18–21, 34, 43

E
European Championships, 7, 8

F
Freedman, David, 8

G
Galiyeva, Rozalia, 31, 43

H
Hill, Kelli, 18, 20
Huilan, Mo, 34

I
International Gymnast magazine, 8
International Olympic Committee, 28

K
Karolyi, Bela, 8, 15, 16, 39, 40, 43–44
Kelley, Shannon, 40
Kochetkova, Dina, 31, 34
Korbut, Olga, 4, 16, 22–25, 28

L
Latynina, Larissa, 26–29

M
Magnificent Seven, 4, 20
Marinescu, Alexandra, 31
Miller, Shannon, 18, 30–33, 43

Mishakov, Alexander, 26
Moceanu, Dominique, 18, 31, 43
Moore, Demi, 18

N
Nunno, Steve, 32

O
Odlozil, Josef, 12
Olympic Games (1952), 4
Olympic Games (1956), 26
Olympic Games (1960), 26
Olympic Games (1964), 26
Olympic Games (1968), 10
Olympic Games (1972), 4, 22, 24
Olympic Games (1976), 15–16
Olympic Games (1984), 39–40
Olympic Games (1988), 7
Olympic Games (1992), 7, 18
Olympic Games (1996), 4, 7, 8, 18, 20, 31–32, 34, 36, 43–44

P
Peszek, Luan, 20
Petrick, Larissa, 10
Phelps, Jaycie, 43
Podkopayeva, Lilia, 31, 34–37

R
Retton, Mary Lou, 38–41

S
Strug, Kerri, 8, 18, 42–45
Szabo, Ecaterina, 39

T
Touricheva, Ludmilla, 28

U
United States Olympic Committee, 4

W
Willis, Bruce, 18
World Championships, 7, 20, 26, 32, 36

Z
Zmeskal, Kim, 7, 8